Evelyn

Thanks for Nothing!

by Peter Maloney
and Felicia Zekauskas

SCHOLASTIC INC.
New York   Toronto   London   Auckland   Sydney
Mexico City   New Delhi   Hong Kong   Buenos Aires

To my best friend, Felicia
—P.M.

To my best friend, Peter
—F.Z.

ISBN 0-439-55360-1

12 11 10 9 8 7 6 5 4 3 2 1   3 4 5 6 7 8/0

Printed in the U.S.A.
First printing, October 2003

CHAPTER 1
November First

"Wow!" said Peter and Felicia when they walked into the classroom.

There were pictures of Native Americans, Pilgrims, and turkeys everywhere!

"Where did all of our Halloween decorations go?" asked Felicia.

"They've disappeared!" cried Tobi.

"Maybe somebody stole them!" said Russ Deluca.

"Maybe we're in the wrong room!" said Peter.

"Don't be silly," laughed Mrs. Robinson. "It's November first. Halloween is over. This is the month of Thanksgiving."

CHAPTER 2
November Feast

Mrs. Robinson told the class how the Pilgrims came to the New World on a ship called the *Mayflower*.

"Food was hard to find," explained Mrs. Robinson.

"Why didn't they go to the store?" asked Russ Deluca.

"There were no stores," said Mrs. Robinson. "But they got help from the Native Americans."

The Pilgrims thanked their friends
at a big feast.

"Do not thank us," said the chief of
the tribe. "Thank the sun, rain, and
earth for helping your crops grow."

"The Pilgrims had a lot to be thankful for," said Tobi.

"We do, too," said Mrs. Robinson. "So for Thanksgiving, I want each of you to tell the class what you're thankful for."

CHAPTER 3
Thanks Thinking

Peter and Felicia were walking to school. Thanksgiving was just a few days away.

"Have you decided what you're thankful for?" asked Peter.

"Yes," said Felicia. "What about you?"

"Not yet," said Peter.

"But you have so much to be thankful for," said Felicia.

"I know," said Peter. But he really didn't.

Peter liked questions with answers
that were either right or wrong,
like "What does 2 plus 4 equal?"

He didn't like questions like
"What are you thankful for?"

"How do I know if I'm being thankful
for the right thing?" Peter asked Felicia.
Felicia laughed.

"There are no right or wrong answers,"
she said.

That's the problem, thought Peter.

Peter started carrying a notepad in his pocket.

He wrote in it whenever he thought of something to be thankful for.

Soon he had a long list.

CHAPTER 4
The Circle of Thanks

The day before Thanksgiving finally arrived. The children sat in a circle.

"Lew, let's start with you," said Mrs. Robinson. "What are you thankful for?"

"My parents for taking me to football games," said Lew.

"My dog because he never barks or growls at me," said Rich.

"My cat because she always purrs when I pick her up," answered Patty.

Peter's turn was coming soon.
He reached into his back pocket.
His notepad wasn't there!
There was a big hole in his pocket.

"Russell," said Mrs. Robinson. "What are you thankful for?"

Russ Deluca was sitting next to Peter.
He reached into his pocket and pulled
out a notepad.
"A lot of things!" said Russ.

"I'm thankful for sunny days when I want to play outside and for rainy days when I want to go to the movies. I'm thankful for books and music and baseball."

Peter couldn't believe it.
Russ Deluca was reading his list!
Now what could Peter say when it
was his turn?

"And most of all, I'm thankful I'm not a turkey," said Russ.
Everybody laughed, even Mrs. Robinson.

"Very good, Russell," said Mrs. Robinson.
"Peter, now it's your turn."

CHAPTER 5
Thanks to a Friend

Peter turned white as a ghost.
Everybody was looking at him.

"I . . . I . . . I forget," said Peter.

"That's okay," said Mrs. Robinson.
"We can come back to you."

Mrs. Robinson kept going
around the circle.

"My electric trains," said Cliff.

"My insect collection," said Tobi.

Mrs. Robinson came to the last person in the circle.
It was Felicia.
"I'm thankful for my friends," said Felicia. "Especially my best one."

Peter looked up.
Felicia was looking across the circle—
at him!
And she was smiling.

"Well, Peter," said Mrs. Robinson,
"I guess you're last. Are you ready
to tell us what you're thankful for?"

Peter suddenly knew what he was
really most thankful for.
And it hadn't been on his list.

"Yes," said Peter.
"I'm thankful for my best friend."
He smiled across the circle at Felicia.